12013

Grandad's Ashes

Walter Smith

Jessica Kingsley Publishers
London and Philadelphia

First published in 2007
by Jessica Kingsley Publishers
116 Pentonville Road
London N1 9JB, UK
and
400 Market Street, Suite 400
Philadelphia, PA 19106, USA

www.jkp.com

Library of Congress Cataloging in Publication Data
A CIP catalog record for this book is available from the Library of Congress

British Library Cataloguing in Publication Data
A CIP catalogue record for this book is available from the British Library

ISBN: 978 1 84310 517 6

Printed and bound in the People's Republic of China by
Nanjing Amity Printing Co., Ltd
APC-FT4814

For Melanie,
whose Grandad it was

When Grandad died, eighty-three people went to the funeral.

A lot of them cried.

Jessica, Colin, Sasha and Tom thought of the good times they'd had with their Grandad. They knew they would miss him a lot.

"He had always wanted to be cremated," said Grandma, "and his last wish was to have his ashes scattered in his favourite place."

After the funeral Grandma was given an urn containing Grandad's ashes. She took it home with her.

"Now then," she said, "I wonder where he would have liked them to go?"

Colin was looking through a trunk of Grandad's old belongings.

He found some of his things from the Navy. These made him think of all the exciting stories Grandad used to tell about his life at sea.

"Why don't we take the ashes onto the water?" he suggested.

So next morning they all went down to the big lake.

It was a windy April day and the water was choppy. Even the ducks stayed safely on the bank.

Grandma and the children clambered into the boat and tried to row to the middle of the lake.

But before they could get halfway there...

Tom began to feel sick.

Then Sasha felt sick.

Then Colin felt sick (although he pretended he didn't).

Then Jessica and Grandma felt sick.

So they all went home with the ashes.

The children next went to stay with Grandma on a hot summer day.

They played hide and seek. Sasha was hiding in a corner of the shed when she found an old tennis racquet.

She remembered when she used to play tennis with Grandad in the park. He always used to let her win!

"Oh! Grandad's ashes!" she thought. "Why don't we sprinkle them on the tennis courts?"

And she rushed to tell Grandma.

So that afternoon they went for a walk in the park.

"This is where we used to play tennis," said Grandma, "but the courts have gone now."

"Let's sprinkle the ashes right here," said Sasha, excitedly.

Just as they were opening the urn they heard a little bell ringing and an angry voice shouting.

"Oi! Keep off my flowers, you lot!"

It was the park keeper, chasing them on a bike!

So they all ran home with the ashes.

It was autumn when they next stayed with Grandma.

One evening they sat down to a huge dinner.

"Delicious carrots, Grandma!" said Colin, as he gulped them down.

"They were planted by Grandad in his vegetable plot last year," said Grandma.

Tom began to think of the summer evenings he had helped Grandad water his plants. He missed him a lot.

"Oh! Grandad's ashes!" he exclaimed. "We can take them there – that was one of his favourite places!"

So after dinner they went out to the vegetable plot. But they found no vegetables – just weeds everywhere.

"Ouch!" said Sasha as she was stung by a nettle.

"Whoops!" cried Jessica as she tripped over some rubble.

"Aargh!" shouted Colin as he was chased by a mouse.

And Tom was sad because he couldn't even find the watering can.

So they all went back indoors with the ashes.

Winter arrived and the children stayed at Grandma's for New Year's Eve.

One afternoon they were having a cup of tea and eating mince pies.

"Remember the time when we sat under that big oak tree and Grandad told us a story about a giant mince pie?" said Jessica.

"Oh yes," said Grandma, "you laughed and laughed!"

Jessica sprang to her feet. "Grandad's ashes!" she cried. "Let's take them there!"

"Splendid idea!" said Grandma.

So they all went for a bike ride to the big oak tree.

But when they arrived, it was gone!

All they could see were houses and shops and cars and lorries.

"Oh dear," said Jessica, "we couldn't tell stories here."

"Pardon?" said Grandma, as a lorry thundered past. "I can't hear you!"

"Never mind," said Jessica.

And they all cycled home with the ashes.

In the spring there was a big fair in town.

From her window Grandma could see a huge balloon that was taking people into the air.

It reminded her of the time Grandad did a parachute jump.

He had been blown off course and ended up on someone's roof!

This gave her a little idea.

Next day the weather was perfect, so they took a trip in the balloon.

Grandma gave the children the urn of ashes to carry.

They went up so far that they were closer to the clouds than the ground.

Suddenly, a gust of wind blew the balloon and knocked everybody off their feet.

"Careful!" cried Grandma. "Hold on!"

They tried not to drop the urn, but the lid fell off and the ashes poured out.

They drifted slowly down to the ground, like magic powder.

Some drifted over the big lake.

Some drifted onto the flowers in the park.

Some drifted onto the overgrown vegetable plot.

And some drifted over the houses and shops and cars and lorries.

When Grandma and the children got home they talked about Grandad for a long time, until the moon came up and it was time for bed.